Bob and Tom

written & illustrated by **Denys Cazet**

A Richard Jackson Book · Atheneum Books for Young Readers

New York   London   Toronto   Sydney   New Delhi

atheneum

ATHENEUM BOOKS FOR YOUNG READERS
An imprint of Simon & Schuster Children's Publishing Division
1230 Avenue of the Americas, New York, New York 10020
Copyright © 2017 by Denys Cazet
All rights reserved, including the right of reproduction in whole or in part in any form.
ATHENEUM BOOKS FOR YOUNG READERS is a registered trademark of Simon & Schuster, Inc.
Atheneum logo is a trademark of Simon & Schuster, Inc.
For information about special discounts for bulk purchases, please contact Simon & Schuster Special
Sales at 1-866-506-1949 or business@simonandschuster.com.
The Simon & Schuster Speakers Bureau can bring authors to your live event. For more information or
to book an event, contact the Simon & Schuster Speakers Bureau at 1-866-248-3049 or visit our website
at www.simonspeakers.com.
Book design by Lauren Rille
The text for this book was set in ITC American Typewriter.
The illustrations for this book were rendered in mixed media.
Manufactured in China
0517 SCP
First Edition
10 9 8 7 6 5 4 3 2 1
CIP data for this book is available from the Library of Congress.
ISBN 978-1-4814-6140-5
ISBN 978-1-4814-6141-2 (eBook)

For Pat and Cheri Cannon

6:45 a.m.

Bob and Tom sat in the farmer's yard.
The sky was dark and stormy.
"I guess the sun isn't coming today," said Tom.
"Nope," said Bob. "Rain's comin'."
Tom agreed. "Yep."

It rained.

"It's wet," Tom noticed.

"It's the water," Bob explained.

Bob jumped up!
"We need to find some dry spots!"

Tom jumped up! "Where?"

"Anywhere!"

Tom looked down. He saw two dry spots.
"There!" he said. "See? Dry spots. One for
you and one for me."

Bob and Tom sat down.

The rain stopped. The sun came out.

"So," said Tom. "What do you want to do today?"

10:19 a.m.

Tom pecked at some corn.

Bob stared at Tom.

Tom stopped pecking. "What's the matter?"

"Nothing." Bob shrugged. "I was just thinking."

"About what?"

"Your head."

"Is it gone?" Tom asked.

"No," said Bob. "I was just wondering
 if there was anything up there . . .
 you know, on the inside."

"There must be something in there!"

"Really? How do you know?"

"I'll look," said Tom. He closed his eyes.
 He looked in toward the middle.

"It's dark in there! I can't see anything."

"I knew it!" Bob gasped. "It's empty!
 No wonder I have to think of everything.
 You don't even need a head!"

"Don't be silly," said Tom. "If I didn't have a head,
I wouldn't have a place to put a hat."

"How true," said Bob. "I should have thought of that."

2:33 p.m.

Tom and Bob walked down the dirt road.
The sun was hot. The air was muggy. They saw
the farmer's grandchildren swimming in the pond.
"That looks like fun," said Tom. "Let's jump in
and cool off."

"What?" Bob cried. "Jump in?
Do you want to sink?"
Tom watched the children
swimming in the pond.
"They're not sinking!"
"Of course not!" Bob declared.
"They're wearing suits that swim."
"Suits that swim?"
Bob sighed. "Why do you think
they're called swimming suits?"
"Oh," Tom muttered. "I didn't know."
Bob shook his head sadly. "I have to
think of everything," he complained.

Tom pointed at the farmer's house.
"I saw a suit that swims hanging on the
farmer's clothesline. I will get it!"
Tom ran fast!

He ran to the clothesline and grabbed Mrs. Farmer's swimming suit.
He ran back so fast that he crashed into Bob. They fell into the pond.

"Help!" Bob cried. "Help! Help! We're not wearing
suits that swim!"
Tom saw Mrs. Farmer's swimming suit.
"There!" he yelled.
"I see it! It broke into two pieces, a part for you
and a part for me. Put it on before we sink!"

"Whew!" Bob wheezed. "That was close!"

"No kidding," said Tom.

5:15 p.m.

Tom and Bob picked some peas in the farmer's garden. Bob stopped pea picking. He looked sad.

"What's the matter?" Tom asked.

"My name," said Bob. "I had it a minute ago, and now it's gone!"

"Where did you leave it?"

Bob tried to remember. "I don't know."

"What did it look like?"

"It was small like yours." Bob sniffed.

"And it had a round thing in the middle."

"Like mine?"

"Don't you remember?"

"No," said Tom. "I must have left mine
with yours."

Tom and Bob looked in the potato patch. They looked under the farmer's beehives. They could not find their names. "Maybe they were stolen," Bob suggested.

"Ask the cow," said Bob. "Ask her if she's
seen our names."

"Excuse me," said Tom. "Have you seen anyone
with names that don't belong to them?"

"What did they look like?" asked the cow.

"They were small," Tom explained, "and they had
a round thing in the middle . . . like a doughnut."

"What kind of doughnut . . . plain, glazed, jelly,
or old-fashioned . . . Any sprinkles?"

"I forgot," said Bob.

"Nope," said the cow. "Sorry."

They searched everywhere.
They asked and asked.
But no one had seen any
names that didn't belong
to them.

The two turkeys crossed the
road and plopped down in
the shade of an old oak tree.

"How sad," Bob moaned. "When we had names we were somebodies,
  but now, our names are gone and we're nobodies."
"We must be somebodies," said Tom. "I can see you. Do you see me?"
"Of course!" Bob said. "But . . . who are you? Who am I talking to?
  Without a name I can't see the who in you!"

"Maybe we need new names," Tom suggested,
"something to put back the who."

"Like what?"

"Well," said Tom. "I could call you Bob."

"Oh!" Bob cried. "That's a wonderful name."

"Yes," said Tom, "and it has a doughnut in the middle."

"I'll call you Tom," said Bob. "That name has a
doughnut in the middle too."

"Plain or glazed?" Tom asked.

"Plain," said Bob. "Mine is glazed."

Bob and Tom walked proudly down
the road with their new names.

7:14 p.m.

After dinner, Bob and Tom
watched the sun go down.
"There it goes," said Tom.
"Yep," said Bob. "Just like always."
Tom nodded. "I wonder why."

"Why?"

"Yes . . . why? Why does the sun come up
in the morning and go down at night?"

"In the morning," Bob explained, "the sun
is full of hot air. So . . . it rises, like a
balloon. By the end of the day the air
is used up, and so, it sinks."

"It has a leak?" Tom asked.

"The sun is old," Bob said. "It takes all
night to refill it."

"Where?"

"At the gas station."

"Wow," said Tom. "You are so smart."

"I know," Bob agreed. "We are what we are."

"I know something too," said Tom.

"Really?"

"Yep! I know what we're going to do today."

"At last!" Bob remarked. "What?"

"Sleep."

"Oh, right!" Bob agreed. "So . . .

what do you want to do tomorrow?"